W9-BYJ-722

BIRD TALK

Overheard by
ANN JONAS

Greenwillow Books, New York

The "bird talk" in this book is based on words used by the people who study birds to help us hear and remember bird songs. These words are called "memory phrases."

The mockingbird, like the one who flies through this book, can repeat the songs of many birds. Listen to what they all have to say.

WIDE-A-WAKE!
WIDE-A-WAKE!

HIYAH HIYAH HIYAH HIYAH
HIYAH HIYAH HIYAH HIYAH

HA, HA, HA, HA
HOO, HOO, HOO,
HA-OO-OO
HEY AL!
HA-HA-HA-HA-HAAH-HAAH
WIDE-A-WAKE!

WHEW
WHEW
WHEW
DEAR!
DEAR!
DEAR!
GO-OUT
GO-OUT
GO-BACK
GO-BACK
MEOW
KIT-KIT-KITTER-KITTER
QUIT
KIT!
KITTY-GO

KITTY
KITTY
KITTY
MEOW
KITTY-KITTY-KITTY

CHEWY-CHEWY-CHEWY
CHEW-CHEW-CHEW
EAT-IT-ALL
EAT-IT-ALL
EAT-IT-ALL

PLANT-A-SEED, PLANT-A-SEED
DROP-IT, DROP-IT
COVER-IT-UP, COVER-IT-UP
PULL-IT, PULL-IT
EAT-IT-ALL, EAT-IT-ALL
CHEW-IT, CHEW-IT
GOBBLE
GOBBLE
GOBBLE

THIEF!
THIEF!
THIEF!
THIEF!
THIEF!
THIEF!
THIEF!
TUT
TUT
TUT

WEE SEE, WEE SEE, WEE SEE
OOOH, POOR SAM PEABODY, PEABODY, PEABODY

YOU SEE IT,
YOU HEAR IT,
YOU KNOW IT,
YOU FEEL IT,
WHAT OF IT?
YANK
YANK
DEAR,
DEAR,
TOO
TRUE!
YANK
YANK
TO WHAT
WHAT
WHAT
WHAT?
CHEERILY-CHEER-UP!
CHEERILY-CHEER-UP!

HERE HERE HERE TURTLE TURTLE TURTLE
YANK YANK YANK YANK

3
x8
TEACHER
TEACHER
TEACHER
TEACHER
THREE
EIGHT
TEACHER
TEACHER
TEACHER
TEACHER

CHECK!
SEE, SEE, SEE,
ISS BEECHER,
EASE, PLEASE,
PLEASED
O MEET'CHA
TO REALLY
READ IT,
TO REALLY,
REALLY
READ IT

CAR!
CAR!
CAR!

CAR! CAR! CAR! CAR! CAR! CAR! CAR! CAR! CAR! CAR! CAR! CAR! CAR! CAR! CAR! CAR! CAR! CAR! CAR! CAR! CAR! CAR! CAR! CAR! CAR!
CAR! CAR! CAR!
WEE SEE
SEE SEE SEE

OH SEE HERE,
SEE ME UP HERE,
WAY UP HERE,
JOHNNY JOE AND JIM
PRETTY, PRETTY, PRETTY
OH, OH, SEE, SEE,
WHAT-A-PRETTY
LITTLE-BIRD-I-BE

PETER
PETER
PETER
HERE
HERE
HERE
JUST-LOOK-AT-ME!
JUST-LOOK-AT-ME!
SWEET, SWEET, SWEET
I'M SO SWEET

SWEET
SWEET
CHEW
CHEW
CHICK-A-DEE-DEE-DEE
CHEW
CHEW
CHEW
CHEW
CHICK-A-DEE-DEE-DEE
SWEET
SWEET
CHEW
CHEW

WHAT-CHEW
WHAT-CHEW
BIRDY-BIRDY-BIRDY?
CHICK-A-DEE-DEE-DEE
PICK
PICK

TEA-KETTLE
TEA-KETTLE
TEA-KETTLE
TEA
MAIDS, MAIDS, MAIDS
PUT ON YOUR
TEAKETTLE-ETTLE-
ETTLE-ETTLE
DRINK YOUR TEA
DRINK YOUR TEA

TEA-KETTLE
TEA-KETTLE
TEA-KETTLE
TEA
PORK,
BEANS

QUICK, QUICK!
HELP, HELP!
FIRE, FIRE!
DEAR
DEAR
DEAR

HURRY
WORRY
FLURRY
BLURRY
QUICK, QUICK!
HELP, HELP!
FIRE, FIRE!
EEK!
WHERE?

SIP SIP SIP
PHEW!
GLUG GLUG GLEEE
HOT-DOG-PICKLE-ICKLE-ICKLE
PORK, BEANS

WHO-
COOKS-
FOR-
YOU?
WHO-
COOKS-
FOR-
YOU-ALL?
WHO-COOKS-
FOR-YOU?
WHO-COOKS-
FOR-YOU-ALL?
BOB-WHITE!

OH, WHO ARE YOU?
WHO ARE YOU ALL?
SLEEP!
SSSHH!

WHO'S AWAKE?
ME TOO!
WHO'S AWAKE?
ME TOO!

THE BIRDS

Some birds have more than one song. When a bird sings a second song, it is listed on the appropriate page.

Jacket
Hiyah, hiyah, hiyah, hiyah—**HERRING GULL**
Check!—**RED-WINGED BLACKBIRD**
Cheerily-cheer-up! Cheerily-cheer-up!—**AMERICAN ROBIN**
To really read it, to really, really read it—**MAGNOLIA WARBLER**
Quick, quick! Help, help! Fire, fire!—**INDIGO BUNTING**
Oh, who are you? Who are you all?—**BARRED OWL**
Bird talk, bird talk—***MOCKINGBIRD***
What-chew, what-chew, birdy-birdy-birdy?—**CARDINAL**

Pages 2-3
Wide-a-wake!—**SOOTY TERN** and ***MOCKINGBIRD***

Pages 4-5
Hiyah, hiyah, hiyah, hiyah—**HERRING GULL** and ***MOCKINGBIRD***
Ha, ha, ha, ha, hoo, hoo, hoo, ha-oo-oo—**COMMON LOON**
Hey Al!—**RAZORBILL**
Ha-ha-ha-ha-haah-haah—**LAUGHING GULL**
Wide-a-wake!—**SOOTY TERN**

Pages 6-7
Whew, whew, whew. Dear! Dear! Dear!—**GREATER YELLOWLEGS**
Go-out, go-out, go-back, go-back—**WILLOW PTARMIGAN**
Meow—**GREY CATBIRD**
Kit-kit-kitter-kitter—**EASTERN KINGBIRD**
Kitty-go—**BLACK RAIL**
Quit kit!—**SANDERLING**
Meow—**REDHEAD**
Kitty-kitty-kitty—**LITTLE TERN** and ***MOCKINGBIRD***

Pages 8-9
Chewy-chewy-chewy, chew-chew-chew—**AMERICAN REDSTART**
Eat-it-all, eat-it-all, eat-it-all—***MOCKINGBIRD***
Plant-a-seed, drop-it, cover-it-up, pull-it, eat-it-all, chew-it—**BROWN THRASHER**
Gobble, gobble, gobble—**WILD TURKEY**

Pages 10-11
Thief! Thief! Thief!—**BLUE JAY** and ***MOCKINGBIRD***
Tut, tut, tut—**AMERICAN ROBIN**
Wee see, wee see, wee see—**BLACK-AND-WHITE WARBLER**
Oooh, poor Sam Peabody, Peabody, Peabody—**WHITE-THROATED SPARROW**

Pages 12-13
You see it, you hear it, you know it, you feel it, what of it?—**RED-EYED VIREO**
Yank, yank—**RED-BREASTED NUTHATCH** and ***MOCKINGBIRD***
Dear, dear, too true!—**MOURNING WARBLER**
Yank, yank, to what, what, what, what?—**WHITE-BREASTED NUTHATCH**
Cheerily-cheer-up! Cheerily-cheer-up!—**AMERICAN ROBIN**
Here, here, here, turtle, turtle, turtle—**KENTUCKY WARBLER**

Pages 14-15
Three, eight—**YELLOW-THROATED VIREO**
Teacher, teacher, teacher, teacher—**OVENBIRD** and ***MOCKINGBIRD***
Check!—**RED-WINGED BLACKBIRD**
See, see, see, Miss Beecher, please, please, pleased to meet'cha—**CHESTNUT-SIDED WARBLER**
To really read it, to really, really read it—**MAGNOLIA WARBLER**

Pages 16-17
Car! Car! Car!—**FISH CROW** and ***MOCKINGBIRD***
Wee see—**ACADIAN FLYCATCHER**
See see see—**GOLDEN-CROWNED KINGLET**

Pages 18-19
Oh see here, see me up here, way up here, Johnny Joe and Jim—**NORTHERN ORIOLE**
Pretty, pretty, pretty—***MOCKINGBIRD***
Oh, oh, see, see, what-a-pretty-little-bird-I-be—**VESPER SPARROW**
Peter, Peter, Peter, here, here, here—**TUFTED TITMOUSE**
Just-look-at-me! Just-look-at-me!—**AMERICAN GOLDFINCH**
Sweet, sweet, sweet, I'm so sweet—**YELLOW WARBLER**

Pages 20-21
Chick-a-dee-dee-dee—**BLACK-CAPPED CHICKADEE**
Chew, chew, chew, chew—**TENNESSEE WARBLER**
Sweet, sweet, chew, chew—**INDIGO BUNTING** and ***MOCKINGBIRD***
What-chew, what-chew, birdy-birdy-birdy?—**NORTHERN CARDINAL**
Pick—**DOWNY WOODPECKER**
Pick—**PURPLE FINCH**

Pages 22-23
Tea-kettle, tea-kettle, tea-kettle, tea—**CAROLINA WREN** and ***MOCKINGBIRD***
Maids, maids, maids, put on your teakettle-ettle-ettle-ettle—**SONG SPARROW**
Drink your tea, drink your tea—**RUFOUS-SIDED TOWHEE**
Pork, beans—**COMMON NIGHTHAWK**

Pages 24-25
Quick, quick! Help, help! Fire, fire!—**INDIGO BUNTING** and ***MOCKINGBIRD***
Dear, dear, dear—**BLACK-THROATED BLUE WARBLER**
Hurry, worry, flurry, blurry—**SCARLET TANAGER**
Eek!—**ROSE-BREASTED GROSBEAK**
Where?—**RED-EYED VIREO**

Pages 26-27
Sip, sip, sip—**BLACK-THROATED BLUE WARBLER**
Phew!—**VEERY**
Glug, glug, gleee—**BROWN-HEADED COWBIRD**
Hot-dog-pickle-ickle-ickle—**RUFOUS-SIDED TOWHEE**
Pork, beans—**COMMON NIGHTHAWK**
Who-cooks-for-you? Who-cooks-for-you-all?—**BARRED OWL** and ***MOCKINGBIRD***
Bob-white!—**COMMON BOBWHITE**

Pages 28-29
Oh, who are you? Who are you all?—**BARRED OWL**
Sleep!—**DARK-EYED JUNCO**
Ssshh!—**BARN OWL**
Who's awake? Me too!—**GREAT HORNED OWL** and ***MOCKINGBIRD***

For Christine

I am grateful to the many bird-watchers who have worked to translate bird songs into phrases understandable to human ears, and especially to the following books and their authors.

Beginner's Guide to Birdwatching, by Todd A. Culver, consultant, and Paul M. Konrad, contributing writer (Lincolnwood, IL: Publications International, Ltd.,1991).

Bird Songs in Your Garden (A Cornell Laboratory of Ornithology Book Album), by Arthur A. Allen and Peter Paul Kellogg (Boston, MA: Houghton Mifflin Company,1963).

Book of North American Birds (Pleasantville, NY: The Reader's Digest Association, Inc.,1990).

Field Book of Eastern Birds, by Leon Augustus Hausman (New York, NY: G. P. Putnam's Sons,1946).

A Field Guide to the Birds East of the Rockies, Fourth Edition (The Peterson Field Guide Series), by Roger Tory Peterson (Boston, MA: Houghton Mifflin Company,1980).

Songbirds and Familiar Backyard Birds, Eastern Region (National Audubon Society Pocket Guide), text by Wayne R. Petersen, prepared and produced by Chanticleer Press, Inc. (New York, NY: Alfred A. Knopf, Inc.,1996).

Watercolor paints and black pen were used for the full-color art.
The text type is Futura.
Greenwillow Books, a division of William Morrow & Company, Inc.,
1350 Avenue of the Americas, New York, NY 10019.
www.williammorrow.com Printed in Singapore by Tien Wah Press
First Edition 10 9 8 7 6 5 4 3 2 1

Library of Congress Cataloging-in-Publication Data
Jonas, Ann.
Bird talk / by Ann Jonas.
p. cm.
Summary: Portrays a variety of birds and their calls, using the "memory phrases" that birdwatchers have devised to help them hear and remember birdsongs.
ISBN 0-688-14174-9 (trade). ISBN 0-688-14173-0 (lib. bdg.)
1. Birds—Juvenile fiction. [1. Birds—Fiction.
2. Birdsongs—Fiction.] I. Title. PZ10.3.J725Bi
1999 [E]—dc21 98-13309 CIP AC

DATE			